The Ugly Pumpkin

For Chloe, Lucy,
Zach and Nate

ISBN-13: 978-0-545-20914-4
ISBN-10: 0-545-20914-5

12 11 10 9 8 7 6 5 4 3 2   9 10 11 12 13 14/0

Printed in the U.S.A.   40

First Scholastic printing, October 2009

Design by Gina DiMassi
Text set in Barbera Fat
The art was done with cut paper, charcoal and colored pencils.

The UGLY PUMPKIN

by

dave horowitz

SCHOLASTIC INC.
New York Toronto London Auckland
Sydney Mexico City New Delhi Hong Kong

I

am the ugly pumpkin,
as you can plainly see.
Of one hundred thousand pumpkins,
none are quite like me.

Since early in October
I've been waiting to get picked,
but each time things start looking up . . .

I end up
getting tricked.

A skeleton came for pumpkins
one bright and crispy day.

Going
MY WAY?

I asked if I could
get a ride . . .
He laughed and said:

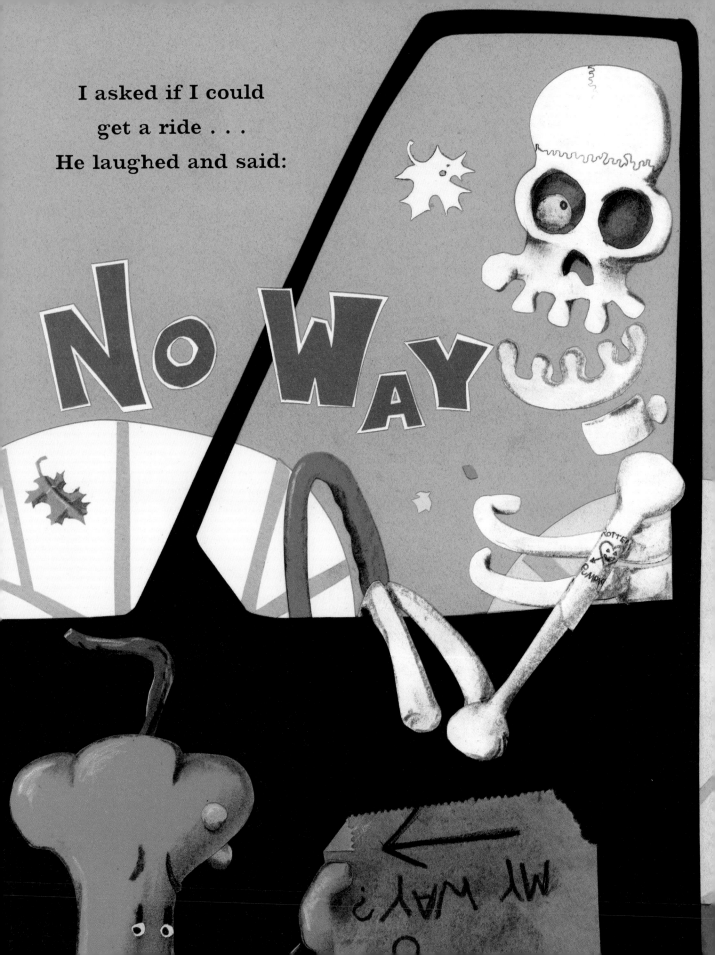

And when I said,
"It's getting late,
and I don't have a home."
He rolled his eye,
said, "Good-bye,"

and left me
all alone.

So I walked into November,
where I happened on some trees.
I asked if I could stay awhile,
and this time I said:

The trees all
started smiling,
and then one
finally spoke:

"Take off yer boots
and spread yer roots . . ."

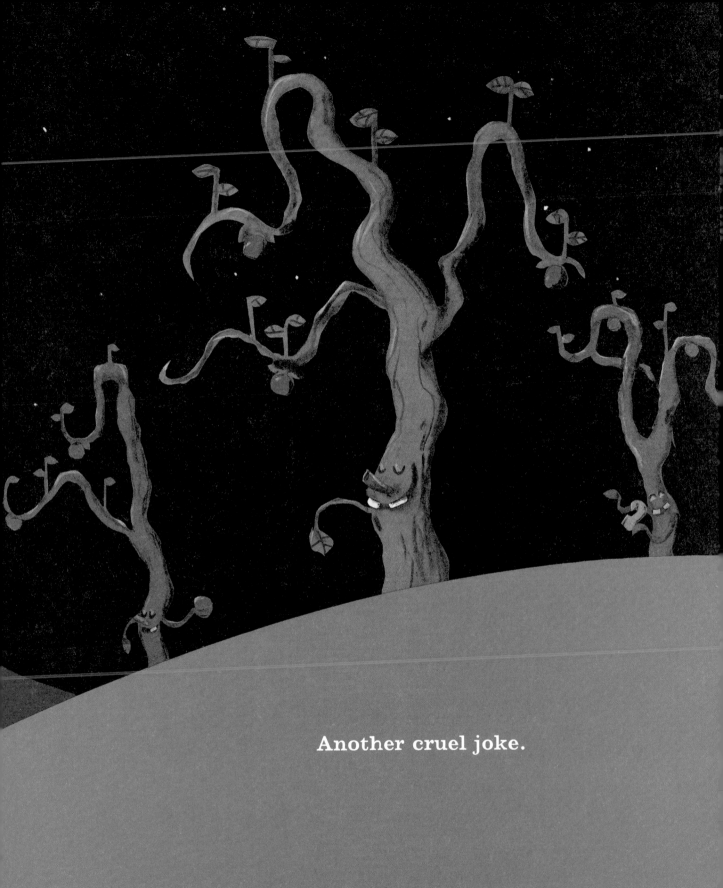

Another cruel joke.

I AM THE UGLY PUMPKIN!

I shouted to the sky.

And then it started raining,
so I began to cry.

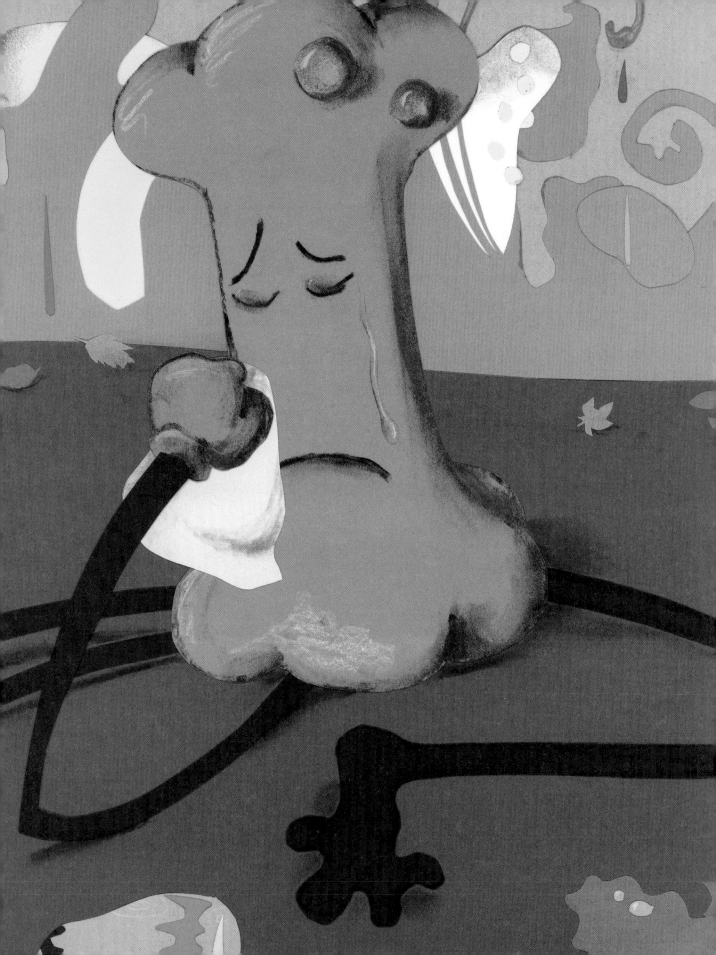

I took shelter in a garden
that was overrun with squash.

I noticed something
very odd
and then thought,
O my gosh . . .

O my
gosh

At last it was Thanksgiving
and I found where I fit in.
Now you know my story,
so let the feast begin.